Where We I

Spain

Donna Bailey

RSVP
**RAINTREE
STECK-VAUGHN**
P U B L I S H E R S
The Steck-Vaughn Company

Austin, Texas

Hello! My name is Adela and
this is my little brother Juan.
We live in Seville, in southern Spain.
We are wearing our best clothes
because today is a special holiday.

Seville is a big city with
many parks and important buildings.
Hundreds of years ago, the Moors of
North Africa came to Spain.
They built many beautiful buildings
in Seville.

Today many of the houses in Seville
are built in the Moorish style.
The arches, doorways, and windows of the houses
are decorated with mosaics
in different patterns.

Our house is in a small courtyard
off a side street.
The trees in the courtyard help
keep the house cool in the summer
when the weather gets hot.

After school we often go to
the Maria Luisa Park near our house.
We like to feed the white doves
in America Square.

In the evening, men often come
to the park to play a game
called bowls.

Sometimes we rent a rowboat and
row around the Plaza de España
which is also in Maria Luisa Park.

8

The Cathedral of Seville with its high tower
was built hundreds of years ago.
The Cathedral is the largest in Spain.
Christopher Columbus is buried here.

Horse-drawn carriages wait just outside
the Cathedral.
Tourists often take a carriage ride
around the city.

Many tourists visit the Golden Tower
on the riverbank.
The Golden Tower was once part of
an old wall that protected the port
of Seville.

Boats still come up the river
to the port of Seville.
In the early morning, fishers
cast their nets to catch fish
in the river.

12

Sometimes we visit my cousins who
live on a farm in the country.
We usually stop to eat lunch on the way.
In the summer, we sit outside to eat
because it is too hot to stay indoors.

The farm is not far from Seville.
My uncle raises sheep and
a few goats.

My cousin has a pet goat.
It is a baby that
lost its mother.
My cousin takes care of it and
feeds it milk.

My aunt makes cheese from the goats' milk.
She presses the cheese into round baskets.
Later she will sell the cheese
in the market in Seville.

16

My favorite festival in Seville is
the April Fair.
Before the fair, a city of tents appears
on the fairground just outside the city.
The tents are set up in rows with little streets
between them.

During the three days of Seville's
April Fair, girls dress in a
special dress.
They wear a scarf around their neck and
flowers in their hair.

The men and horses look their best, too.
Some horses have embroidered saddles
and decorated bridles.

Most men wear a short, black jacket and
a stiff-brimmed gray or black hat.
Many men also wear decorated leather
leggings over their pants.

Some couples ride horseback together.
The woman sits behind her partner and
puts one arm around the man's waist.
Some women ride their own horse and
wear a costume similar to the men's.

The horses and riders parade up and down
the streets in front of little canvas booths
called casetas.
Each caseta belongs to a group of friends
or a business.

The streets of the fairground are decorated
with lights, flags, and flowers.
Cars are not allowed, but the streets are full
of open carriages.

Sometimes a whole family crowds
into a carriage for a ride around
the fairground.

The mules pulling the carriages
are decorated with flowers
and garlands.

Other families ride together on horses.
These people are on their way
to the carnival rides.

There are many carnival rides
at the fairground.
After riding a real horse,
riding a horse on the merry-go-round
is easy.

Some children enjoy the thrills and
bumps of a ride in a bumper car.

The older girls walk up and down
the sidewalks in front of the casetas.
They stop to visit with friends and talk
about what they will do in the evening.

People in the street clap out
a dance rhythm.
Two women begin dancing a flamenco.
They stamp their feet to the rhythm.

Inside each caseta, dancers
will dance the flamenco until late
at night.
They click their fingers and castanets
to the rhythm of the music.

Even young children are allowed
to stay up late during the April Fair.
The singing and dancing go on
almost all night.
No one thinks of going to bed before
4:00 in the morning!